The
Littles
and the
Big Storm

BY **JOHN PETERSON**
PICTURES BY **ROBERTA CARTER CLARK**

SCHOLASTIC INC.
New York Toronto London Auckland Sydney

There are more books about the Littles
you may want to read:

The Littles
The Littles Take a Trip
The Littles Have a Wedding
The Littles Give a Party
   (Former title: *The Littles' Surprise Party*)
Tom Little's Great Halloween Scare
The Littles and the Trash Tinies
The Littles Go Exploring
The Littles to the Rescue
The Littles and Their Friends

All Littles books are published in paperback
by Scholastic Book Inc.

ISBN 0-590-42276-6

12 11 10 9 8 7 6 5 4 3 2   9/8 0 1 2 3/9

To Roberta,
for always picturing the Littles
just as they are, and for suggesting
what might happen to them
in a big storm.

Tom and Lucy Little were on the Biggs' roof before anyone else in the family.

"If they don't get up here soon," said ten-year-old Tom, "they'll miss seeing Cousin Dinky land the glider."

"*Della* is going to land the glider," said eight-year-old Lucy.

"She *is*?" asked Tom. "You're kidding."

"She told me she was," said Lucy. "Cousin Dinky does all the take offs and she does all the landings."

"But landing is *harder*!" said Tom. "Especially on a roof."

"So what?" said Lucy.

"Dinky's a better pilot," Tom said.

"He is not!" said Lucy.

"He's flown lots longer than Della," Tom went on.

Lucy shrugged. "So what?" she said.

"Golly, Lucy, is that all you can say — 'So what?'" said Tom.

Lucy was standing on the highest part of the roof near the chimney. "There they are!" she shouted. "There's the glider."

"Where?" Tom looked all around.

"See?" Lucy said. "Near the tall sycamore tree by the pond."

Tom nodded. "I see them now."

"They're coming awfully fast," said Lucy.

"It's the wind from the big storm," Tom said.

Lucy looked up at the sky. "I don't see the storm," she said. "I thought it was supposed to come tomorrow."

"The wind always comes up like this before a big storm," said Tom.

Lucy yelled into the wind, "Hooray for Cousin Dinky and Della!"

"What are you yelling for?" asked
Tom. "They can't hear you. The wind is
blowing this way."

"I like to yell," Lucy said. "The Biggs
are on vacation. We can yell as loud as
we want."

"Hey, that's right," said Tom. He
grinned. Then he began to yell too.

When the Biggs were home, the
Littles had to worry about being heard
or seen by them. That was because *both*
families lived in the house, but the Biggs
didn't know it.

TOM   LUCY   MR. LITTLE

The Littles were a tiny family. (The biggest Little was just six inches tall.) They were so tiny that the whole family could live secretly inside the walls of the house owned by Mr. and Mrs. Bigg.

There were nine Littles in the family: Tom and Lucy; their parents, Mr. and Mrs. William T. Little; their baby sister, Betsy; Granny and Grandpa Little; and two uncles. The Littles' ten-room apartment was comfortable, with plenty of room for everybody.

There were many other tiny families living in the Big Valley. Many lived in houses just as the Littles did. Some lived in hollowed-out trees. Others lived in underground burrows. Some, called

MRS. LITTLE   BABY BETSY   GRANNY

UNCLE PETE   UNCLE NICK   GRANDPA

Brook Tinies, lived near the stream that passed by the Biggs' house. And finally, there were the Trash Tinies, who lived in their own city under the town dump.

Not *one* of these tiny people had ever been seen by a regular-sized person. The tiny people would have looked strange to an ordinary person. The tiny people were not only very small, they had tails.

The tails weren't useful. Tiny people couldn't hang by them or wag them. But they were handsome tails, and the tiny people kept them brushed.

The tiny families didn't visit one another often. They lived too far away from each other. So they kept in touch by mail.

DELLA   AND   DINKY

Cousin Dinky Little was the glider pilot who delivered the mail. He and his wife, Della, flew up and down the Big Valley, carrying the mail and having adventures.

Usually they dropped the Littles' mail into a net stretched across the chimney. But today was not Mail Day. The two adventurers were landing on the roof, not flying by. And when the wind blew hard, they sometimes needed help getting the glider tied down. Tom and Lucy knew what to do if they were needed.

The blue and white glider drew near the Biggs' roof. Two parachutes snapped open behind it. They acted like a brake to slow it down.

At the same time, a fish-hook anchor was dropped from the cockpit. The anchor was tied to a piece of twine. The glider bounced to a landing on the roof. The fish hook caught on a shingle and pulled the glider to a halt.

Tom and Lucy ran forward. They jumped onto the wing tips of the glider to hold them down.

Cousin Dinky leaped out of the cockpit and tied the glider to the roof.

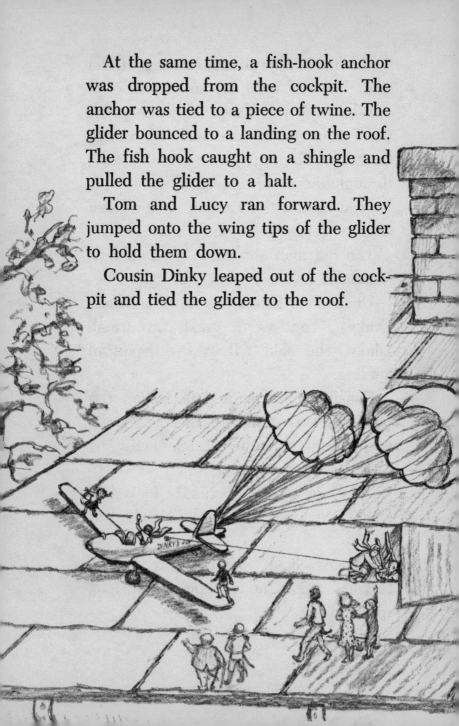

"That was a beautiful landing," Della said, "even if I do say so myself."

While this was happening, the rest of the Littles got to the roof. All except Grandpa. He was just now climbing through the secret shingle-door.

"You missed the landing, Amos," said Granny Little to her husband.

The old man shrugged his shoulders. "Someone has to be last," he said.

Uncle Pete shook hands with Cousin Dinky. "You were great, as usual, Dinky," he said. "It was a beautiful landing."

Cousin Dinky pointed to Della, who was still sitting in the cockpit. "Della was flying the glider, Uncle Pete," he said.

"Oh?" said Uncle Pete. He looked at Della. "Not bad," he said. "Not bad at all."

"Uncle Nick!" said Della as she climbed from the cockpit. "You look splendid!"

Uncle Nick was dressed in his best uniform. He was wearing all of his medals. The tiny soldier was once a major in the Mouse Force Brigade. Major Nick had recently retired after serving thirty years fighting mice in Trash City. That was the tiny people's town in the city dump.

"Uncle Nick," said Mr. Little. "Do you think you should wear your best uniform? Aren't you afraid you'll tear it or something?"

"I *always* wear my best uniform when I go into battle," Uncle Nick said. "As soon as I heard there were more mice than usual in the town dump this spring, I began polishing my medals. I knew I'd be called into active duty for the emergency."

"You look very handsome," said Mrs. Little, who was holding Baby Betsy in her arms.

"We'd better get going, Uncle Nick," said Cousin Dinky. He was looking at the sky. "The weather report is bad. The storm may get here sooner than expected."

"The storm has already hit the coast," Mr. Little said. "The radio says it's as strong as ever and still heading this way."

"What a poor time for the Biggs to take a vacation," said Granny Little. "I feel sorry for them. I wonder if they'll be coming back because of the storm."

"I don't think they will," said Mr. Little. "We'll have to be ready to repair any damage to the house — if we can."

"Well, it's a little excitement for the rest of us anyway," said Grandpa.

"Oh, Grandpa!" said Mrs. Little. "What a thing for *you* to say! You just came back from an exploring trip after being shipwrecked for two years. How much excitement should a person of eighty-four have?"

"All he can get!" said Grandpa.

"You know — I think you actually *miss* being on that island," Mrs. Little went on.

"It's those young friends of his he misses," said Granny Little. "The Brook Tinies who were shipwrecked with him."

"All aboard, everyone!" said Della. She climbed back into the cockpit.

"Good-bye, Nick," said Uncle Pete. "Give those mice the devil for me."

Uncle Nick and Cousin Dinky took their seats in the glider.

"It's off to an exciting adventure for the three of them," said Uncle Pete, "and the same dull stay-at-home life for the rest of us."

"Fasten your seat belts," Cousin Dinky called out. Then: "All set!"

With that, Mr. Little and Uncle Pete unhooked the fish-hook anchors that held the glider in place.

The glider began to roll down the

roof. It picked up speed quickly. Just as the glider got to the edge of the roof, Cousin Dinky raised the wing flaps. The glider rose into the air. It zoomed out over the Biggs' yard.

"Hurrah!" yelled the Littles on the roof.

"Hurrah!" yelled the Littles in the glider.

"They're off!" said Granny Little. "God bless them."

The tiny blue and white glider sailed away from the house. It circled, riding the breezes higher and higher. Finally, when it was above the trees, Cousin Dinky turned the glider back toward the house.

As it passed high overhead, the tiny people on the roof could see the three adventurers waving down to them. In a few moments the glider was out of sight on its way to the town dump.

The next morning Tom and Lucy ran into the living room.

"It's here!" said Tom. "The storm is here."

"It's not so much," said Lucy, disappointed. "I thought it would be terrible."

Mr. Little and Granny Little were sitting in the living room with Uncle Pete.

Uncle Pete wagged his finger at the children.

"You kids better stay off that roof," he warned. "The wind in a big storm can blow you away."

"It's nothing like that, Uncle Pete," said Tom. "Really. Just rain. Lots of it."

"It'll get worse, Tom," said Mr. Little. "What you were looking at is just the edge of the storm."

"Is that all we're going to get?" Lucy asked. "Just the *edge* of the storm?"

"No," said Mr. Little. "I'm sorry to say we're going to get the whole thing. I turned on the Biggs' radio this morning. The storm, they say, is one of the biggest, and it's going to go right over us."

Tom and Lucy hugged one another and jumped up and down.

"Oh good!" said Lucy.

"It's traveling slowly and dumping lots of water," Mr. Little went on.

Lucy clapped her hands. She looked up. "Tom — it's going right *over* us," she said.

Granny Little took a deep breath. "I wish the Biggs were here," she said.

"Did you children see anything of Jimmy Rodgers when you were on the roof?" Mr. Little asked.

Tom shook his head. "I didn't see him," he said.

"Nope," said Lucy.

"That boy just isn't responsible," said Mr. Little.

"When George Bigg hired him, I said it was a mistake," said Uncle Pete. "They've been on vacation for three days now and the kid hasn't shown up."

Grandpa came into the room. "I heard what you were saying," he said. "What's the boy supposed to do?"

"Feed Hildy, the cat, while the Biggs are gone," Mr. Little said. "The food is in the refrigerator. All he has to do is come in when he's supposed to and do it. Mr. Bigg gave him a key."

"Why don't we let Hildy out?" suggested Tom. "She can find her own food."

"Do you mean *mice*?" said Lucy. "Yuk!"

"Why not open the refrigerator and get the cat food?" said Grandpa.

"Grandpa!" said Uncle Pete. "With that heavy door?"

"Oh, it can be done, I think," said Grandpa. He sat down and closed his eyes.

"Shhhh!" said Granny Little. "Your Grandpa is thinking."

Grandpa opened his eyes and stood up. "Hildy can open the door herself," said Grandpa. "First, tie a strong piece of twine to the cat. Then tie the other end to the door of the refrigerator."

Tom shook his head. (Tom had tamed Hildy and he was the family's cat expert.) "She won't pull the door open," he said. "Even if I sit on her back and dig my heels into her. She's strong enough, I think — but you can't get cats to do things like that."

Grandpa held up his hand to silence Tom. "Tie another piece of string to her catnip mouse. Place the mouse on the floor in the next room — near the door, but where Hildy can't see it," he said.

The old man stopped. He looked around at everyone.

Tom began to grin as the idea came to him.

"Lucy will be hiding on the other side of the door opening," Grandpa went on. "At the right moment she'll *pull* the catnip mouse across the door jamb!"

". . . and Hildy jumps for the mouse, yanking the door open," Tom finished.

Lucy leaped to her feet. "Let's do it, Tom!" she said.

"Grandpa," said Tom. "Why don't you come with us?"

"Yes, Amos, why don't you?" said Granny Little. "You wanted something exciting to happen. Here it is."

Grandpa leaned back in his chair. "No," he said. "I don't see anything exciting about *doing* it. The problem has been solved." The old man stretched his arms and yawned.

Tom and Lucy were in the kitchen with Hildy the cat. Tom was sitting high up on Hildy's back. Everything had been set up as Grandpa suggested.

There was a small cardboard box on the floor near the refrigerator. Tom meant to jam the box in the door opening as soon as Hildy opened it.

"Are you ready, Lucy?" Tom called.

"All set," answered Lucy. She stood behind the door to the living room. She held the string that was tied to the catnip mouse.

"Now!" said Tom.

Lucy pulled the string with all her might.

The catnip mouse scooted across the door opening.

At the same time, Tom dug his heels hard into Hildy's back.

The cat sprang forward, pulling at the twine.

The door opened slightly!

Tom slipped off the cat's back. He stuffed the cardboard box into the door opening. "It worked!" he yelled. "Hey, Lucy! It worked!"

Lucy came running up. "Oh, Tom," she said, "that was neat!"

Tom untied the twine that held Hildy to the refrigerator door.

Lucy peeked into the refrigerator. "How can we give Hildy her milk?" she asked. "Look how large those containers are. Should we poke a hole in one?"

"No," said Tom. "The cat food will be enough. She can drink water."

The two children climbed into the refrigerator. They searched the lower shelf. There was an orange, half a can of apricots, and some leftover potato salad.

"It's cold in here," said Lucy. "We should have worn our coats."

They climbed to the second shelf. Behind the eggs and next to some mustard sauce they found the cat food. It was covered with plastic wrap.

Just then they heard a scratching noise. It was somewhere in the house.

"What's that?" asked Lucy.

Tom listened. "Sounds like a key in a lock," he said. Then: "Oh, oh! Let's get out of here."

Too late. Someone was in the kitchen.

"Here, kitty! Come here, Hildy!" It was a boy's voice.

"Jimmy Rodgers!" whispered Tom.

"Tom — what'll we do?" said Lucy.

"We can't go out there," said Tom. "He'll see us."

"Hey, there you are," said Jimmy. "Are you hungry?"

"Meow!" said Hildy.

Jimmy saw the refrigerator door. "What's this doing open?" he said.

Then: "This is nutty. There's a box jammed in here." He pulled the box from the door opening.

Tom and Lucy were frightened. They stood next to the cat food, wondering what to do.

"I'll get your food, Hildy," said Jimmy Rodgers.

Tom and Lucy hid behind a purple eggplant. When Tom peeked out, he saw a huge hand coming toward him. Scared, he backed up and fell into a bowl of jello.

Jimmy picked up the dish of cat food.

It went pitch black inside the refrigerator as the door closed.

"Tom! Where are you?" It was Lucy calling.

"Over here! I fell in some jello."

"Yuk!" said Lucy. She felt her way in the dark, following Tom's voice.

"This way, Lucy," Tom called.

The bowl of jello was slippery and wobbly, but Tom finally got out of it.

"Tom, it's terribly dark in here. What happened to the light?"

"It goes out when the door is shut," said Tom. "It's okay — I have a candle." The tiny boy took the stub of a birthday candle from his pocket. He lighted the candle with the one small match he always carried.

Lucy looked around. "Tom," she said, "this is awful. We're locked in."

"We're not exactly *locked* in," said Tom. "This refrigerator door is held shut by magnets."

"Can we open it?"

"Probably not," said Tom. "The magnets are too strong for tiny people."

"I wish we were big kids so we could get out of here," Lucy said.

"If we were big kids we wouldn't be *in* here," Tom said. "We'll just have to wait until Jimmy Rodgers is gone, then we'll try and push the door open."

"Oh, Tom!" said Lucy. "What'll we do if we can't get the door open?"

"Don't worry," said Tom. "Someone will miss us. They'll come to get us out."

"Will they know we're here?"

"Sure," said Tom, trying to talk bravely. "Where else would we be? Dad knows we went to feed Hildy."

"But when he sees Hildy's been fed,"

said Lucy, "he'll think we did it, and we're someplace else playing, won't he?"

"Golly, that's right," said Tom.

"I guess we should yell for Jimmy Rodgers to open the door," said Lucy.

Tom shook his head. "We can't do that," he said. "No big person must *ever* see a tiny person. It's a law!"

"But, Tom!" Lucy began to cry. "We'll *die* in here, won't we? I don't want to die."

Tom stared long at the candle. Then he said: "I guess you're right. If we don't get Jimmy to help us, we may never get out of here. Let's yell."

The two children began to shout. "Help! We're in the refrigerator! Let us out! Help!"

They kept on shouting for a few minutes.

Nothing happened. The door didn't open.

"He can't hear us," Tom said.

"Why not?"

"The doors on these things are made to keep the cold in — they're insulated," said Tom. "I guess it keeps the noise in too."

"I'm freezing, Tom," said Lucy. She held her hands over the candle flame.

"Careful of that candle, Lucy," said Tom. "I don't have another match."

"I wish I'd worn my coat," Lucy said.

The two children sat down on the glass shelf. Tom fixed the candle to the shelf in front of them. He put his arm around Lucy to keep her warm.

Lucy's teeth chattered.

After a while they tried to push the door open. It wouldn't budge.

"What are we doing?" shouted Tom. He leaned forward quickly and blew the candle out. "I'm crazy! I just remembered."

"What did you do that for?" asked Lucy. "It's dark again."

"The flame was burning up the oxygen in the air," Tom said.

"What's wrong with that?" asked Lucy. "Don't all candles burn oxygen?"

"Sure," said Tom. "But there's only so much oxygen in the air in this refrigerator. When it's used up, we won't be able to breathe."

Lucy began to cry softly. So did Tom. They sat in the cold and dark holding onto each other and crying. They sat there for a long time.

Suddenly the door opened and the light came on in the refrigerator.

"Tom! Lucy!" It was Mr. Little. "Are you in there?"

"Daddy!" yelled Lucy.

"We're here, Dad," said Tom, quickly drying his eyes.

When they were out of the refrigerator and on the kitchen floor, Tom said: "How did you know we were in there, Dad?"

"I saw Jimmy Rodgers coming in the house," said Mr. Little. "Uncle Pete and I came down to see what was going on. We got here just in time to see him pull the box out of the door. I knew you were in there."

"We would have got you out sooner," said Uncle Pete, "but we couldn't get that cat away from the cat food."

"Then how did you get the door opened?" asked Lucy.

"We used this wooden ruler," said Uncle Pete. He pointed to a twelve-inch ruler by the refrigerator door.

"We pried the door open," said Mr. Little. "We used the ruler like a lever. It was surprisingly easy."

"Daddy," said Lucy, hugging her father. "I was *so* scared."

"I know, sweetheart," Mr. Little said. "It's all over now."

"And, Daddy," Lucy went on, "do you know what happens when the refrigerator door is shut? The light goes out, that's what!"

The rain fell all day. The wind grew stronger. That afternoon two groups of Littles looked around the house for damage. They met in the Littles' living room.

Uncle Pete said: "Tom and I found a leak in the roof."

"There's water getting into the attic," Tom added.

"Is it something we can fix?" Mr. Little asked.

"I hope so," Uncle Pete said. "It's where the chimney goes into the roof. There's a hole at the seam and the water is getting through."

Grandpa, who was dozing in his chair, mumbled something.

"What did you say, Amos?" asked Granny Little. "Speak a little louder. You know I'm hard of hearing."

Grandpa opened one eye. "Use bubble gum to fill the hole," he said.

"Good idea," said Uncle Pete.

"Tom and I know where Henry Bigg has some," said Lucy.

"It's a big hole," Tom said. "It will take at least half a piece of bubble gum to fill it. Who's going to chew all that gum?"

Grandpa opened the other eye. "Take it up on the roof to soften it in the rain," he said. "Then jump up and down on it to get it 'chewy' enough."

"Oh dear," said Mrs. Little. "You'll get that sticky gum all over your shoes."

"Take *off* your shoes," said Grandpa. He closed his eyes.

Tom nodded his head. "And gum is sticky when it's only a little wet," he said. "With all that rain, you don't have to worry about that, Mother."

"Can't we chew a little piece *ourselves*?" said Lucy. "Golly!"

Uncle Pete, Mr. Little, Tom, and Lucy climbed out on the roof to repair the leak. Mrs. Little and Granny Little went to the attic to see what they could do about the water there.

Grandpa Little said he would snooze in his chair. That is, if no one minded. The project didn't look very interesting to him.

Mrs. Little and Granny found water on the attic floor near the chimney. It was still dripping from the ceiling. They got a dish and shoved it under the leak.

The tiny women began sopping up the water on the floor. They used old

rags that Mrs. Bigg had put in a plastic bag.

"I know Mrs. Bigg wants these rags used to do jobs like this," said Mrs. Little, "because I watched her when she sorted them out."

"Hold that one!" Granny Little said. She stopped Mrs. Little from using one of the rags. "That's a nice piece of cloth. I can cover a chair with it," she said.

Granny Little folded the cloth and laid it in a dry place.

As they worked, Granny kept finding pieces of cloth that she needed for other things. "This would make a nice dress for Lucy," she said, and "Now wouldn't this make a dandy shirt for Tom," and "I know Peter would love a bathrobe made from this."

She folded each piece of cloth and placed it with the others in a neat pile.

She found a pair of overalls that had been on one of Henry Bigg's GI Joe dolls. (Henry was the Biggs' only child.) She held the overalls up to look at them. "With a tuck here and there I can shorten these for Amos," she said. They went on the pile.

At about this time Mrs. Little heard a noise. It came from the other end of the attic.

"I don't hear it," said Granny Little. She cupped her ear and listened. "But then, I don't hear much anyway."

"There it is again," said Mrs. Little, lowering her voice. "It sounds like someone or something moving around over there."

"It must be one of the family," Granny Little said. "Shall we give them a call?"

"Everyone's on the roof," said Mrs. Little, "except Grandpa."

"And he's sleeping in the living room," said Granny Little, who was whispering now.

"What should we do?" asked Mrs. Little.

"Tell the others," said Granny Little.

Mrs. Little was already walking away. In the dark she didn't see the coat hangers scattered about the floor. They tripped her up. She fell to the floor, making a loud noise. The noise at the other end of the attic stopped suddenly.

The two women tiptoed toward the secret shingle-door in the roof. They climbed through. Mr. Little and the others had just finished repairing the hole in the roof.

When they heard what had happened, everyone went to the attic. They looked everywhere, but they didn't hear the noise, and they couldn't find anything that might have made it.

Suddenly Granny Little called: "Come here, everyone!"

The Littles came running from every part of the attic. Granny pointed to the place where she had piled the pieces of cloth.

They were gone!

The next day it was still raining hard. Mr. Little went to the roof to see what was happening outside. Uncle Pete looked around inside.

Mrs. Little asked Tom and Lucy to take out the trash. They had just left when Mr. Little came back.

"The pond is right up to the top of its banks," Mr. Little reported. "The creek is overflowing. And the full force of the storm isn't even here yet!"

Uncle Pete came in. "Water is beginning to trickle into the cellar," he said.

"Oh dear!" said Mrs. Little.

"I thought that would happen sooner or later with all this rain," Mr. Little said. "Whenever there's a hard rain for three or four days, some water comes into George Bigg's cellar."

"This storm shows no sign of stopping," said Uncle Pete.

"Don't worry," said Mr. Little. "If too much water gets in the cellar, the sump pump starts automatically and pumps it out."

"A flood would make a mess on the cellar floor," said Mrs. Little.

"And ruin the furnace," added Uncle Pete.

"Yes," said Mr. Little. "But as long as the water is pumped out as it comes in, there will be no damage to the furnace or the hot-water heater."

Granny Little was listening. She said: "Just the same, I dearly wish the Biggs were home. I'd feel a lot better about it if they were."

"They must have heard the news of the storm," said Mr. Little. "Perhaps they are already on their way."

Uncle Pete looked around. "Where are the children?" he asked. "They should be told to stay away from the roof and the cellar."

"They're taking out the trash," said Mrs. Little. "They went upstairs just before you came in."

"Upstairs!" Mr. Little said. "You've forgotten. They shouldn't take out the trash in the usual way when the Biggs aren't here."

"Oh, that's right," said Mrs. Little. "They love to do it the usual way. I'm sorry. I wasn't thinking."

"I'll take care of it," Uncle Pete said. He started for the door. "Just be kind enough to have a cup of hot coffee waiting for me when I get back."

Meanwhile Tom and Lucy were under the floorboards of the second floor, walking on the downstairs ceiling. They were carrying the trash in two plastic film containers. (Mr. Bigg used a lot of film to take pictures. He always threw the containers away and the Littles saved them.) When they got to a spot over the kitchen — and directly over the sink — they stopped.

"Me first!" said Lucy.

"I'd *rather* be last," Tom said. "I can aim better after I see what you do."

Tom got down on his knees. He pulled a plug out of the floor (which was really the kitchen ceiling). Tom looked through the hole. Six feet below he could see the kitchen sink. And there was the target! The garbage-disposal hole in the sink.

"Okay, Lucy," said Tom. "Bombs away!"

Lucy emptied her film container full of trash into the plug-hole. The children watched it tumble through the air. It landed right in the center of the garbage-disposal hole.

"Bull's-eye!" said the children as the trash disappeared down the hole in the sink.

"I always wondered," Tom said, "how Grandpa knew exactly where to cut this hole."

"How did he, Tom?" asked Lucy. "I've forgotten."

"He says he'll explain it to me when I'm older," said Tom. "It has something to do with mathematics, I think."

"Anyway, Grandpa invented a good way to get rid of the trash," said Lucy. "It's fun."

"He didn't do it for fun," Tom said. "It's just smart not to take chances where the Biggs might see you."

A few minutes later the children were gone, and Uncle Pete was standing on the kitchen counter. He went to the sink and found the switch that turned on the garbage-disposal unit. He turned it on. There was a loud noise as the Littles' trash was ground up.

"Sometimes that sounds like a fierce growling animal," thought Uncle Pete.

Just then, out of the corner of his eye, Uncle Pete thought he saw something running on the kitchen floor.

He wondered if it was only his imagination.

That afternoon Tom and Lucy went to the Biggs' living room to look at television. They turned the set on and sat together on the huge couch.

It was a treat for the Little children to get this close to the TV set. When the Biggs were home they had to hide nearby if they wanted to watch. And they had to look at the programs the Biggs chose.

Today Tom and Lucy were watching their favorite afternoon program. It was a series of stories about a family. There were two children — a girl and a boy — and they lived with their parents and an uncle.

During a commercial, Tom climbed up to the TV set and turned the dial. Suddenly there were some sad-looking people talking about operations, automobile crashes, and dying. "That's a soap opera," said Tom.

"What's a soap opera?" asked Lucy. "I thought an opera was when people sang the story."

"You can always tell a soap opera," Tom went on, "because whenever you turn it on something terribly sad is going on."

"Tom — remember the time they had a TV show about tiny people?" Lucy asked.

"Yeah," said Tom. "Boy — was that awful!"

"They didn't even have tails," said Lucy.

"And they *talked* to big people," added Tom.

"That could never happen in real life," said Lucy.

Tom turned the TV back to the other program. They sat looking for a while. Then, all of a sudden, the television set went off.

"That must be from the storm," said Tom. "I guess the electricity got knocked out. Maybe it'll come right back on."

The two children sat quietly. They listened to the sounds of the storm outside. After a while Lucy said: "Maybe it's not the storm. Maybe there's something wrong with the TV."

"I'll check and see if the lights go on," said Tom. He climbed up on the back of the sofa. He reached up and turned the wall light switch on. No lights.

"It's the electricity for sure," Tom said.

Just then they heard a loud "PSSSSSSSTT!" It came from the kitchen.

"Hildy is spitting," said Lucy. "She's angry." Lucy stood up on the couch trying to see into the kitchen.

The cat gave a loud "MEE-OOOWWW!!"

The tiny children slid down off the couch. They ran to the kitchen.

Hildy was trying to get in behind the refrigerator. The space wasn't large enough for her. She kept sticking her paw in between the wall and the refrigerator.

"What is it, girl?" Tom asked. He turned to Lucy. "There must be something back there."

"Let's not go back there," said Lucy. "It might be an animal or *something*."

"We'd better tell Mother and Dad," said Tom.

Lucy pointed to the floor. "Look!"

There was a small blue feather lying at her feet.

The electricity was on again before Tom and Lucy got back to the apartment. They told everyone what had happened.

"Something strange happened in the kitchen this morning too," said Uncle Pete. "I thought it was my imagination, but now. . . . " He told how he had seen something running.

"It seems we have a mystery on our hands," said Mr. Little.

"Oh dear," said Mrs. Little. She held her hand to her head. "I hope I'm not going to get a headache over this. Mysteries make me nervous."

"Now, Mother, don't get upset," said Tom.

"I hope it's not mice," Lucy said.

"Mice!" said Mrs. Little. "Oh dear!"

"Where is Amos?" asked Granny Little. "He's awfully good at solving mysteries."

"Oh, he's taking a nap," said Uncle Pete. "He says the sound of the rain on the roof makes him sleepy."

"What your mother said reminds me," said Mr. Little to Tom and Lucy, "that we are almost finished with our aspirin tablet. With the Biggs away, it's a good time for you to get another one."

"Okay, Dad," said Tom. "Come on, Lucy." He started for the door, then stopped. "Should we take a weapon with us? You know, because of the mystery?"

"Oh those nasty weapons!" said Granny Little. "Must we get them out? Someone's going to get hurt."

"No, Tom," said Mr. Little. "I don't think we've seen anything that shows we need to be too worried. Just be careful, that's all."

The two tiny children walked through the wall passageways that led to the bathroom. One of the tiles in the bathroom was really a secret door for tiny people. The children opened the door and climbed through to the bathroom counter.

Tom found the aspirin on the counter along with toothbrushes, shaving cream, and other things.

"We're lucky this time," Tom said. "Remember the time we had to climb into the drawer?"

"It's my turn to open it," said Lucy.

"I'll get it into the right position," said Tom.

The tiny boy pushed the flat aspirin tin next to a jar of cold cream. Lucy climbed up on top of the jar.

"Now be sure and land on the right place," said Tom, "or it won't open."

"I know, I know," said Lucy. "Golly, you don't have to tell me how to open an aspirin tin."

Lucy stood for a moment on the edge of the jar lid. Then she jumped. She landed on the tin where it said 'press to open.' The other end of the aspirin tin popped up.

"Good," said Tom. He picked up one

of the aspirin tablets. He rolled it on the counter like a wheel. It rolled toward the sink. The aspirin tablet ran into a puddle of water and began to dissolve.

"Oops!" said Tom. "We'll have to get another one."

"You've made a mess, Tom," said Lucy. The tiny girl walked to the sink. "Hey — there's a mess here already. There's water in the sink and puddles all over the counter."

"Water in the sink?" said Tom. He walked over. "That's impossible. I *saw* Mrs. Bigg check the bathroom just before they left. There wasn't any water in it then."

Lucy opened her mouth to say something. A huge clap of thunder stopped her. At the same time the bathroom was filled with the bright flash of lightning.

"Wow!" said Tom. "That almost busted my eardrums. Let's get up to the apartment and tell everyone about the latest mystery."

The big storm had come at last. The sky darkened; the wind screamed; the rain beat hard against the windows; lightning flashed and thunder crashed. The Biggs' house creaked under the full power of the storm.

Uncle Pete came up from the cellar. "She's flooding fast," he said. "The sump pump is not working."

"Not working?" Mr. Little said. "How could that be?"

Tom and Lucy came in with the aspirin tablet. "We've found another mystery," said Tom.

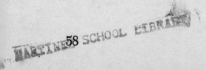

"Later, Tom," said Mr. Little. "We've more serious things to take care of."

"I'd better take a look at that sump pump," said Grandpa coming in from his bedroom. "I was watching when George Bigg had it put in, so I know something about it." The old man smiled and winked at the children. "At least this storm has finally cooked up a little excitement," he said.

"Now, Grandpa — you be careful down in that cellar," said Mrs. Little.

"Let him go," Granny Little whispered to Mrs. Little. "This is just what he needs to perk him up. He's showing an interest in something for a change."

"I suppose that's right," said Mrs. Little. She hurried from the room when Baby Betsy began to cry.

Mr. Little said: "Our tin-can elevator lands in the cellar near the sump pump. We should be able to get at it from there."

"Hold on there, Will," said Uncle Pete. "The flood has covered that up. We can't go down that way."

Mrs. Little came back into the room. She was carrying the baby.

"Good heavens!" said Mr. Little. "The water is up that high already? We've got to do something in a hurry or it will ruin the furnace."

"Well, isn't the pump under the water?" asked Mrs. Little.

"Of course," Mr. Little said. "It's in a shallow pit below the level of the cellar floor. That's how it's able to pump out the water before it fills up the cellar."

"How can you possibly get to the pump then?" said Mrs. Little.

Mr. Little shrugged his shoulders. "I'll have to dive down to it, I suppose," he said.

"The water is muddy, Will," said Uncle Pete. "You won't see much."

"I'll feel around then," said Mr. Little. "That may tell me something."

"Now, Will Little — you listen to me," said Mrs. Little. "Don't you do anything foolish. It's only a furnace you're trying to save."

Grandpa patted Mrs. Little's hand. He spoke softly. "We're going down there to look over the problem, and that's all."

"We'll need some kind of boat or raft," said Mr. Little. "Something that will float — to get across the cellar floor to the pump."

"Henry Bigg's sailboat is on the shelf in his closet," said Tom. "It's a keen boat."

Mr. Little shook his head. "No — by the time we get that heavy boat off the shelf and down the cellar stairs," he said, "it might be too late to save the furnace and the hot-water heater."

"Isn't there a piece of wood lying around in the cellar?" said Grandpa. "Something we could use for a raft?"

"Umph!" said Uncle Pete. "Grandpa — you've forgotten what a neat man

George Bigg is. There's *nothing* lying around his cellar floor."

"Well, there's wood in the workshop out back," said Mr. Little.

"I know something," Lucy said.

"Just a minute, Lucy," said Mr. Little. "Don't interrupt now. We're trying to solve a difficult problem."

"But I have an *idea!*" Lucy said. "We could use Henry's Lincoln logs to make a raft."

"Lucy — that's a good idea!" said Grandpa. "We can drag the logs there piece by piece and put it together on the spot." He thought for a moment. "We'll have to tie the logs together."

"Use rubber bands, Grandpa," said Tom. "Just like you did with your submarine raft."

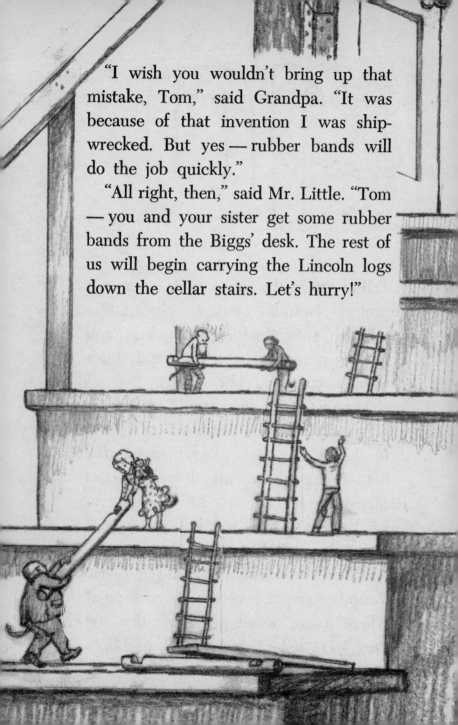

"I wish you wouldn't bring up that mistake, Tom," said Grandpa. "It was because of that invention I was shipwrecked. But yes — rubber bands will do the job quickly."

"All right, then," said Mr. Little. "Tom — you and your sister get some rubber bands from the Biggs' desk. The rest of us will begin carrying the Lincoln logs down the cellar stairs. Let's hurry!"

All of the Littles set to work on the raft project. Grandpa was in charge. He pointed out which Lincoln logs and planks were needed. Tom and Lucy went looking for rubber bands.

The rest of the tiny people carried the logs and planks from Henry Bigg's closet to the cellar. They piled them on the bottom step. Baby Betsy was awake. So Mrs. Little had to carry her in a sling on her back. The baby seemed to enjoy the bouncing around.

When everything was finally in place, the raft was put together. At each point where a log rested across another log they were held together with a rubber band. After a square of logs was put together, the planks were set on top of them like a floor. Larger rubber bands were used to hold the planked floor in place.

While this was going on, Mrs. Little went to the Biggs' kitchen. She found some plastic spoons to use as paddles. At last the raft was in the water. By this time the water was high enough to cover the bottom step.

"All aboard!" said Lucy.

"Not so fast, Lucy," said Mr. Little. "There's not enough room for everyone aboard this raft."

"*I* never intended to go," said Mrs. Little. "Betsy and I will wait here."

"Three people on the raft are enough," said Mr. Little. "Grandpa, Uncle Pete, and I will go."

The cellar lights blinked off and on. The thunder rumbled outside.

Tom was disappointed about not going on the raft. But he didn't make a fuss.

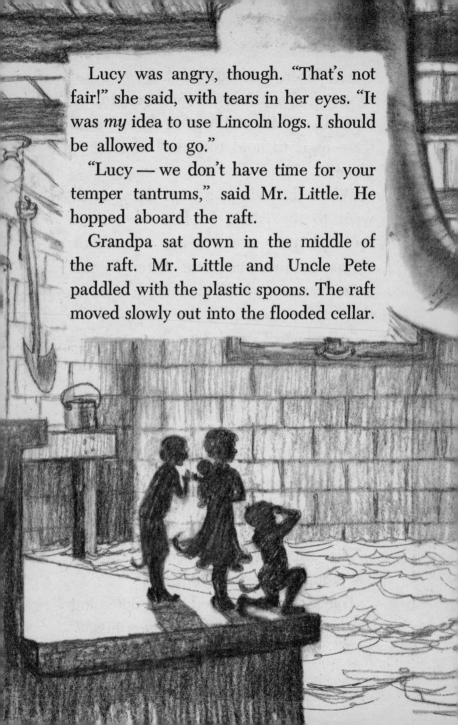

Lucy was angry, though. "That's not fair!" she said, with tears in her eyes. "It was *my* idea to use Lincoln logs. I should be allowed to go."

"Lucy — we don't have time for your temper tantrums," said Mr. Little. He hopped aboard the raft.

Grandpa sat down in the middle of the raft. Mr. Little and Uncle Pete paddled with the plastic spoons. The raft moved slowly out into the flooded cellar.

It headed for the other side of the room.

"I hope they don't take any chances," said Mrs. Little. "It's just not all that important."

"We have to do our best to take care of the house when the Biggs are away," said Granny Little.

"Oh, I suppose you're right," said Mrs. Little.

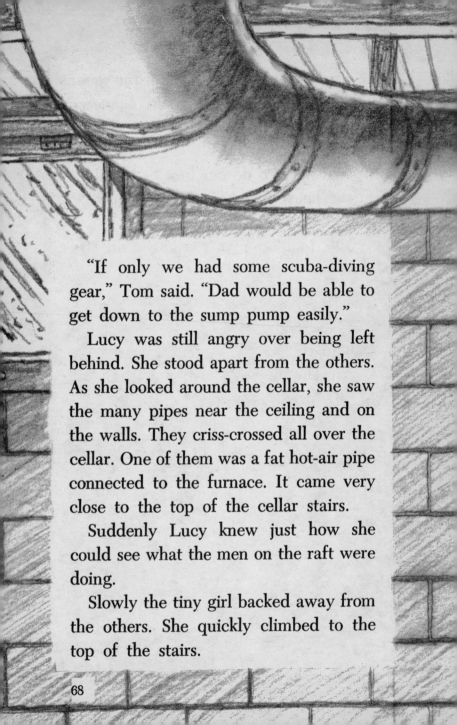

"If only we had some scuba-diving gear," Tom said. "Dad would be able to get down to the sump pump easily."

Lucy was still angry over being left behind. She stood apart from the others. As she looked around the cellar, she saw the many pipes near the ceiling and on the walls. They criss-crossed all over the cellar. One of them was a fat hot-air pipe connected to the furnace. It came very close to the top of the cellar stairs.

Suddenly Lucy knew just how she could see what the men on the raft were doing.

Slowly the tiny girl backed away from the others. She quickly climbed to the top of the stairs.

Now the hot-air pipe was only an inch away. Lucy jumped from the stairs to the pipe.

She made her way along the pipe toward the furnace in the center of the cellar. The pipe was large enough so that a tiny person could walk on it easily. When the pipe got near the furnace, it slanted down from the ceiling. Lucy slid down the pipe.

At this point Lucy was standing on the pipe where it entered the furnace. She was about five feet above the flooded cellar floor. Lucy could see everything. Below and ahead of her was the raft. At the far wall of the cellar Lucy could see the electric fuse box. It was near a black plastic pipe coming out of the water. That was where the pump was, Lucy knew that. Behind her, at the bottom of the cellar stairs, Lucy saw the rest of the Littles. Good! They hadn't even missed her.

But what was that moving at the top of the stairs? Lucy tried hard to see.

Just then the lightning flashed. The thunder exploded right afterward. It sounded like a bomb going off. At the same time the lights went out.

Lucy jumped at the sound. She lost her balance in the dark. Her foot slipped. She reached out to catch herself, but there was nothing to get hold of.

"DADDY!" screamed Lucy as she fell from the pipe.

Mr. Little stood on the raft trying to see into the blackness. "Wasn't that Lucy yelling?" he said. "It sounded as if it came from above us."

"How could that be?" asked Uncle Pete. "We left her back on the cellar stairs."

"Will! Will!" It was Mrs. Little calling across the water. "Lucy isn't here! She's disappeared."

"Great Scott!" said Uncle Pete. "It *was* Lucy! What on earth was she screaming for?"

"Lucy! Lucy!" called Mr. Little. "Where are you?"

No answer.

Mr. Little shouted over to the others. "Stay where you are. It's too dark to move around." Then he said to the men on the raft: "We should have brought some candles. Why didn't we think of that?"

"Let's pray for the lights to come back on," said Grandpa.

"I can't see a *thing*," said Mr. Little. "I've never felt so helpless in my life."

"Will! She's here!" It was Mrs. Little again. "She's here!"

"Thank heavens," said Mr. Little.

"Get Grandpa over here, Will," called Mrs. Little. "There's a surprise here for Grandpa."

"What did she say?" asked Grandpa.

"Says there's a surprise for you," Uncle Pete said.

"Keep yelling," said Mr. Little to Mrs. Little. "We'll paddle toward your voices."

By now the men on the raft were beginning to see dimly in the dark cellar.

The people on the cellar steps kept up a steady yelling to guide them.

Mr. Little laughed. "That's an awful racket," he said.

"I hear a man's voice over there, don't I?" asked Grandpa.

"Impossible," said Uncle Pete. "There's no man there."

When they were almost to the steps, the lights came on again.

"Hurrah!" yelled everyone.

Mr. Little blinked from the bright light. He looked toward the cellar stairs. There were three other tiny people standing there with his family.

One was a tall man wearing overalls too large for him. There were two children standing next to the man. They were dressed in green. One was wearing a green hat with a blue feather. The other child had on the same kind of hat but no feather.

"Oh my goodness — this is too good to be true!" said Grandpa. "Look who's here. My good friends the Brook Tinies have come to visit."

Grandpa jumped off the raft. He hugged the children. Then he said to the man: "Mr. Beck — how did you know I was dying to see Purl and Dewey?"

"Because they were dying to see you," said the children's father. "Ever since coming home from being shipwrecked, they have talked my ear off about visiting you."

Dewey Beck, who seemed about ten years old, said: "We've been wandering around this big house for a couple of days looking for you."

"And they found us just in time," said Mrs. Little. "Just when Lucy fell from the furnace into the water."

"Thank heavens!" said Granny Little.

Purl Beck, about twelve years old, pointed to the top of the stairs. "We were up there," she said, "when we saw Lucy on the hot-air pipe. When the lights went out, she screamed. We heard the splash. Dad dived in and pulled her out."

"In the *dark!*" said Tom.

"I didn't know who was helping me," Lucy said, "and I didn't even care."

Purl said: "House Tinies live in strange places. It's nothing like a cave, and it's not like the tree-stump house. Did you know there's a huge cat in this house? It chased us."

"That's Hildy, our friend," said Tom. "Hey — were you behind the refrigerator in the kitchen hiding from the cat? Did you lose a feather?"

"Refrigerator?" said Dewey. "What's that? Where's the feather?" He felt his hat for the missing feather.

The Littles laughed.

"I think we were in the kitchen when that fierce animal growled at us," said Mr. Beck. "Weren't we, children?"

"Yes," Purl said. "We ran like chipmunks."

Uncle Pete roared with laughter. "Then it was you I saw running away when I turned on the garbage disposal," he said.

"Garbage disposal?" Mr. Beck said. He scratched his head. "We sure have a lot to learn about house living."

Granny Little was looking closely at Mr. Beck. "Where did you get those overalls, Mr. Beck?" she asked.

"These?" said Mr. Beck looking down at his dripping overalls. "They don't fit very well, do they? I found them at the top room in the house the other day when we were searching for you. I put them on because I had ripped my clothes badly on a nail in the wall." He laughed. "You know — when you get a Brook Tiny away from the water he can be clumsy."

"Oh, that reminds me of part of the mystery," said Tom. "Were you swimming in the bathroom sink?"

"We did find a nice place to swim,"

said Mr. Beck. "I guess it was the bathroom. I hope we didn't do anything wrong."

"*We* would have emptied the water when we were through," said Tom.

"So the Biggs wouldn't know," added Lucy.

"Ah, you see — we *do* have a lot to learn," said Mr. Beck.

"Anyway," Mr. Little said, "the mystery is solved. And we're thankful for your help in saving Lucy."

"And we need some more of your help," said Grandpa. He pointed across the flooded cellar and explained the problem.

"What can we do?" asked Mr. Beck.

"Just before the lights went out I saw what was wrong," Grandpa went on.

"How could you?" asked Mr. Little. "The pump is under water."

"It wasn't hard to figure out," said Grandpa. "The cord wasn't plugged in."

"Oh my goodness!" said Mr. Little.

"Mr. Beck and the children are

excellent swimmers," Grandpa went on. "They can dive down under the water and find the plug for us. We'll dry it off and get it up to the outlet by the fuse box where it belongs."

"Very good," said Mr. Little. "It would be wonderful if we could get the cellar dry again before the Biggs get back."

"Do you really want to dry this up?" asked Mr. Beck. "What a shame. This place is beautiful just the way it is."

The Littles laughed.

"Spoken like a true Brook Tiny," said Grandpa.

By the next day the storm was over. The Littles and the Becks spent the morning visiting with each other. That afternoon Cousin Dinky, Della, and Uncle Nick came back from Trash City.

Uncle Nick made a sour face. "We just had three very boring days," he said. "The mice disappeared when the storm came."

"And the storm was no problem at the

dump, either," Della said.

"That city is so well made," said Cousin Dinky, "that the water runs off as easily as it does off a duck's back."

"You should have stayed home," said Grandpa. He winked at Tom and Lucy.

"Yeah!" said Tom. "We had a mystery."

"And a flood!" said Uncle Pete.

"And lots and lots of exciting things happened," said Lucy.

"It was a blessing," said Granny Little. She smiled at her husband.

Two days later the Bigg family came home. Mr. Bigg looked quickly through the house. "It's amazing!" he said to his wife. "There are no problems from the storm. You know, when I first saw that tree knocked down in the yard, I thought . . . but everything inside is all right. Not a broken window or a leak anywhere. And the cellar is as dry as a bone!"